Little Britches
and the
Rattlers

by illustrated by

Eric A. Kimmel **Vincent Nguyen**

Marshall Cavendish Children

Marshall Cavendish Corporation
99 White Plains Road
Tarrytown, NY 10591
www.marshallcavendish.us/kids

Library of Congress Cataloging-in-Publication Data
Kimmel, Eric A.
Little Britches and the rattlers / by Eric A. Kimmel; illustrated by
Vincent Nguyen. — 1st ed.
p. cm.
As Little Britches, in her best attire, starts for the rodeo in town, she
is waylaid by several rattlesnakes wanting to do her harm, but with
some quick thinking she finds a way to outsmart them all.
ISBN 978-0-7614-5432-8
[1. Cowgirls—Fiction. 2. Rattlesnakes—Fiction. 3. Texas—Fiction.]
I. Nguyen, Vincent, ill. II. Title. PZ7.K5648Li 2008
[E]—dc22
2007030155

The illustrations are rendered in graphite, watercolor, and digital.
Book design by Vera Soki
Editor: Margery Cuyler

Printed in Malaysia
First edition
1 3 5 6 4 2

mc Marshall Cavendish
Children

To Harriet and Kalico
—E. A. K.

For Deborah Nix
—V. N.

One fine Texas morning, Little Britches saddled her pony and headed out for the rodeo. She figured she had a good chance to win first prize in the calf-roping contest.

"It's gonna be a fine day," Little Britches said to herself.
"I can feel it down to my boots."

Little Britches took a shortcut through the dry gulch.
She hadn't gone far when a rattlesnake lifted his head.

"Little Britch-ch-ch-es, I'm gonna s-s-swaller you up!" the rattler hissed.

"Aw, Mister Rattler, I'm just a tiny little thing. I'll hardly make a meal for you at all," said Little Britches. "Say—if you let me go, I'll give you my new Stetson hat."

"I've always wanted a Stetson hat," the rattler said. "Hand it over. Now git before I change my mind."

Little Britches gave the rattler her hat. The rattler put it on. Didn't he look sharp!

But Little Britches didn't stick around. She and her pony took off down the gulch. They hadn't gone far when two rattlers slithered out from behind a rock. "Little Britch-ch-ches, we're gonna s-s-swaller you up!"

"Aw, Rattlers, don't do that. If you let me go, I'll give you my doeskin vest and my satin blouse," said Little Britches.

"I've always wanted a ves-ssss-st," the first rattler hissed.

"I've always wanted a blou-sssssssss-se," said the second rattler. "Hand 'em over! Now git before we change our minds."

Little Britches handed over her vest and blouse.
The rattlers slithered inside and buttoned them up.
Didn't they look handsome!

But Little Britches didn't stick around. She galloped away on her pony as fast as she could ride. She didn't get far when three more rattlers crawled out of the dry creek bed.

"Little Britch-ch-ches, we're gonna s-s-swaller you up!"

"Aw, Rattlers, I ain't worth your time! If you let me go, I'll give you each something nice. You can have my new gloves, my blue jeans, and my chaps with the silver conchos."

"Hand 'em over!" the rattlers said. "Now git before we change our minds."

Little Britches handed over her gloves, chaps, and blue jeans.

The rattlers put them on. Didn't they look smart!

But Little Britches didn't stick around. She and her pony took off without taking time to blink.

What did they meet around the bend but a giant rattler—longer and bigger than all the others put together! "Little Britch-ch-ches, I'm gonna s-s-swaller you up," the rattler hissed.

"Well, go ahead and do it," said Little Britches. "Your pals took my clothes. You may as well eat me because I ain't got nothing left to give you."

"What about those fine red boots you're wearing? The ones with the map of Texas on 'em," the rattler said. "I've always wanted a pair of boots like that."

"You can have 'em," Little Britches said. She pulled
off her boots and tossed them to the rattler. "Now I'm
going to the rodeo!" And off she went.

Little Britches rode on, feeling mighty blue. Those rattlers had taken her rodeo clothes. All she had left were her long johns and red bandana. How could she rope calves in long johns? Everybody would laugh at her, even if she won. She might as well turn around and go home.

Suddenly she heard hissing and rattling.
It came from the bottom of a dry water hole.

Little Britches hopped down from her saddle. She crept over to the water hole and peeked over the edge.

What did she see but rattlesnakes! A whole nest of them! They were the same ones who had taken her clothes.

The rattlers were showing off their new outfits and arguing about which was best, getting mad as only a rattler can get.

They got so mad that they threw down their clothes and started chasing each other around in a big circle.

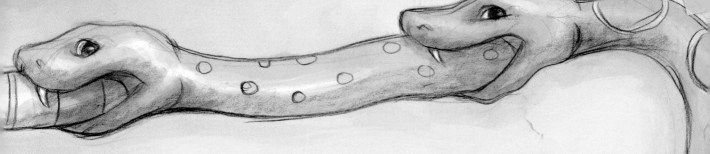

'Round and 'round they went. As Little Britches
watched, they grabbed each other by the tail and
started swallering.

Those rattlers swallered and swallered till they swallered themselves up. They just disappeared. There wasn't a bit left of them—not a fang, not a rattle. Not even a piece of snakeskin. There was nothing at all. Just those fine new rodeo clothes lying on the ground.

"Yippee!" Little Britches let out a whoop.

She pulled on her clothes, leaped into the saddle, and galloped all the way to the rodeo.

She arrived just in time for the calf roping.
And what do you know—she roped her calf in
ten seconds flat and won first prize!

Little Britches got to pick out a
shiny new championship belt
buckle for herself, as big as
a dinner plate.

And which one
did she pick?

Why, the one with the
rattlesnake, of course!